THE FISHING SUMMER

For my family —
HJ, EJ and PJ — TJ

To my wife, Ping —
For encouragement
and support — AZ

Groundwood Books / Douglas & McIntyre
585 Bloor Street West
Toronto, Ontario M6G 1K5

Distributed in the U.S.A. by
Publishers Group West
4065 Hollis Street, Emeryville, CA 94608

The publisher gratefully acknowledges the assistance of the Canada Council
and the Ontario Arts Council.

Library of Congress data is available.

Canadian Cataloguing in Publication Data

Jam, Teddy
The fishing summer

"A Groundwood book".
ISBN 0-88899-285-8

I. Zhang, Ange. II. Title.

PS8569.A427F57 1997   jC813'.54   C96-932190-2
PZ7.J35Fi 1997

The illustrations are done in acrylics.
Printed and bound in China by Everbest Printing Co. Ltd.

THE
FISHING SUMMER

TEDDY JAM

PICTURES BY

ANGE ZHANG

A GROUNDWOOD BOOK

Douglas & McIntyre

VANCOUVER / TORONTO / BUFFALO

WHEN I was a boy my three uncles lived in a big wooden house by the sea. Every summer they painted it white. They had white shirts, too. On Sundays they would do the laundry and hang their white shirts out on the line, where they would flap in the wind like big raggedy gulls.

My three uncles and my mother had been children in that white wooden house. Every summer my mother would take me there for a visit.

My uncles had a fishing boat. It was like a huge rowboat with a little cabin in the middle, hardly big enough to go inside. At the end of the little cabin was the engine.

That engine had started off in a big car. Uncle Thomas, who was the oldest and had a long black beard, had taken the engine out of the car and put it in the boat. Even when it rained and stormed, Uncle Thomas could keep the motor going.

Uncle Rory was the middle uncle. His beard was black, but he kept it short by cutting it with the kitchen scissors. He could look at the sky and tell if it was safe to go out. And when the wind blew up the sea, and the clouds and fog fell over the boat like a thick soupy blanket, Uncle Rory could find the way home.

Uncle Jim was the youngest uncle and my mother's twin. He had no beard at all. He was the fisherman. He had to know where the hungry fish would be, and what they would be hungry for.

At the end of each day I would stand at the dock, waiting. The boat would come in, and my uncles would pick me up. Then we would go to the fish factory. There I would help my uncles load the fish into cardboard boxes to be weighed on the big scale. A giant with little eyes that looked like bright fox eyes would write down the numbers on a piece of paper. Then my uncles would take the paper to the cashier and get paid.

I wanted to go fishing.

"One day," Uncle Jim said, "when you get big."

"No way," my mother said. "You'll fall in and drown."

"I can swim," I said.

"You're only eight years old," my mother said.

"I started going when I was eight," said Uncle Thomas out of his big beard.

"Thomas," said my mother in a sharp voice that made the room go quiet. And I remembered another story. That my grandfather used to fish with his own brothers, and when one of the brothers got hurt, Thomas took his place. A few years later he dropped out of school and started fishing all year round. When my grandfather drowned, my other uncles started going out on the boat with Thomas.

That night I couldn't sleep. I wanted to go fishing so badly. I got dressed, then went down to the dock.

All along the bay you could hear the waves gently splish-splashing, the boats swaying and creaking against the docks. The stars were huge and bright. They hung over the sea like fruit ready to fall.

I stepped from the dock into the boat. It was strange being there alone. I wondered what it would be like to pull off the ropes, drift across the ocean and end up in some country I'd never even heard of.

The rocking of the boat made me sleepy. I went into the cabin and pulled an old blanket over myself.

I woke up to the sound of the motor hammering in my ears. I pushed back the blanket and scrambled out of the cabin. We were at sea!

But the boat was barely moving. My uncles were hauling in huge nets. Soon the boat deck was covered with narrow flopping herring twice the length of my hand, shining and silvery in the sun.

The whole time they emptied the nets into the boat, my uncles pretended I wasn't there, looking right past me, or stepping around me.

Suddenly Uncle Jim pointed at me and shouted, "Stowaway!"

The others looked as though surprised to see me. "Stowaway. Aye, Captain. Throw him overboard."

For just the tiniest little moment I wasn't sure what was going to happen. Then they all laughed and rumpled my hair and patted me on the back as though I'd done some wonderful thing.

"Your mother knows you're here and we promised not to drown you," said Uncle Rory, handing me a knife. "Now all you have to do is earn your keep."

The herring were the bait. I helped Rory cut them up while Thomas headed the boat out past the mouth of the cove. That was the farthest I'd ever been. I could still see my uncles' house, a small patchy white square against the wild heather and grass.

Soon even the cove's mouth had disappeared from view. My uncles drank tea with milk and sugar from their thermoses. They also had a thermos for me. It was filled with hot chocolate. And in the little plastic lunch suitcase my mother had prepared for us was a bag of cookies.

"You see?" Rory said. "You did bring us good luck."

I put my hands in the sea to wash away the fishy smell. In the water my fingers looked white and dead. They came up numb with the cold, and I had to slap my hands together to warm them up.

The waves were going slip-slap against the boat. With each wave the front of the boat rose up. Then it fell down into the trough before the next wave carried it up.

"Feeling sick?"

"I'm fine," I said.

"I always used to puke," Rory said. "Then I started drinking tea. Keeps my stomach down."

"We didn't want to tell you this before you came," Thomas said, "but he might still puke any time. Better stay out of his way." Thomas's big black beard made it hard to know when he was joking.

Suddenly in the middle of the ocean, when we could hardly see the land any more Thomas stopped the boat and threw down anchor. He baited a hook for me, and I began letting out my line.

The idea was to let it right down to the bottom of the ocean, pull it up a few feet, then jig it up and down. In those days millions of cod were parked at the bottom of the ocean, waiting for lunch. When I felt something on the line, I was supposed to wind it up.

The first couple of times I didn't have a fish at the end.

"There's currents at the bottom," Rory told me. "They feel like a fish at first. Wait for a bigger tug."

I waited. I kept getting tugs, but I didn't know if they were bigger. Finally I pulled up the line again. At the end was a huge lump. It was so big I thought it must be a rubber boot. But it turned out to be a fish.

Rory swung it into the boat. It landed with a big thump and just lay there. Thomas attached it to a stringer and put it back in the water.

Meanwhile my uncles were hauling fish up as fast as their arms could go. I kept catching them, but slower. My hands grew sore and red.

Thomas found a greasy old pair of gloves from beside the motor. "Didn't have gloves when we were boys," he said.

"Nope," said Rory. "Dad made us stick our hands in vinegar to make them tough."

On the way back, just outside the cove, we stopped to set the herring nets again. "That way there'll be something here for us tomorrow," Rory explained.

Suddenly he whirled and threw the net out of the boat. It spread into a giant billowing mesh, then slowly settled on the water. But one of the corners got tangled up. Thomas eased about around the net, then as we came close, told me to lean over and grab the wooden float.

As I did, a little wave came up under the boat. A tiny little wave you wouldn't notice unless you'd been stupid and leaned over so far that when the wave came and the boat tipped you slid off the boat into the water.

The water was colder than ice. It filled up my shoes, put its fingers between my toes, quickly soaked my pants and started to drag them down.

I began swimming hard, kicking with all my strength, but I forgot to shout. The boat was moving away when I finally called out. My uncles turned around and saw me in the water.

Thomas cut the motor and Rory held out the paddle to me. I was too proud of my swimming to use it. I splashed right up to the boat, then reached up and grabbed the gunwale.

When I got out, I felt like my fingers had looked—white and numb. Rory grabbed the greasy blanket I'd slept under and wrapped it around me. Then he sat me on his knees and squeezed me till I got warm.

We were one of the first boats home, but my mother was down at the dock, waiting for us. I had taken off the blanket, but my soaking clothes told my mother I'd been in the water.

"How did that happen?" she demanded, glaring at my uncles.

"Now, Edith," Uncle Rory said. The same tone he'd used one Christmas when he caught her cheating at Monopoly.

"Just tell me."

"It was my fault," I said. "I was leaning over the side of the boat and I just fell in."

"Swims a lot better than you used to," Uncle Thomas said. "*He's a natural.*"

He's a natural. Uncle Thomas's voice when he called me that was the purest praise I'd ever heard. He wasn't just saying I was a good swimmer, or a good kid for taking the blame. He was saying I was part of the family. A real fisherman, like him and Rory and Jim and my grandfather's father. Right then, if he would have just asked me, just snapped his fingers, I would have jumped in the ocean and swum forever.

My mother's face turned red again. We walked up to the house. She had made a big old-fashioned tea with cookies and cakes and sandwiches to celebrate the first day fishing.

I went upstairs to change, then came down to eat. "Well," Thomas said to my mother, "aren't you going to be asking him if he enjoyed himself? Now that he's a member of the crew."

"Don't be giving me that," my mother said. "You can wait a few years. Until then he does his swimming in pools and at the beach."

"Don't be making him a baby," said Uncle Rory.

"He's a fisherman now," Jim said.

"He is not!" my mother shouted. "He *is* a baby. He's my baby and you're lucky you didn't drown him."

Uncle Thomas was standing at the counter refilling his cup. Uncle Jim just sat there, looking at my mother as though she were a stranger. Rory, too. The news was coming onto the radio with that funny little crackle it had.

I looked at my mother. She turned away from me. Now my uncles started staring at their feet, as though they'd been caught wearing girls' socks.

"I want to go," I said.

"You're not going anywhere," my mother pronounced.

The next day I was out on the boat again. My uncles were hauling up fish faster than ever. So was I, because my mother was there, helping me and supplying us all with bait.

It was a hot day, and when we got back to the cove the water felt warm on my hand. My mother put her own hand in, to test it. Rory and Thomas were standing at the front of the boat, their big tanned arms folded across their chests, satisfied with the day's work. My mother went and stood between them.

"Great day," she said.

"It was," Rory said. "To tell you the truth, Edith, I didn't know you had it in you."

"Thanks," my mother said. She had her hands on her brothers' backs. Then she gave a push. They hit the water with a giant double splash. I was the one who had to pull them in with the oars. My mother was laughing so hard, she couldn't move.

From that day we both went out with my uncles every day. By the end of the summer my arms had new muscles and my hands were tough as canvas. On the last day my uncles grabbed my mother and tossed her in. She wasn't even surprised. She just took off her boots, heaved them toward the boat, then swam to shore.

It was the last evening before we had to go back for the start of

school. My uncles had caught some lobsters, and that evening we
roasted them in a fire on the shore.

Then they toasted me and said how I'd become a real fisherman.
Uncle Thomas gave me a drink of his coffee. It was bitter and it
was raw and it was sweet. It was the taste of that summer and I
never lost it.